MAR   2009

Finders Keepers

A Viking Easy-to-Read

by **Dori Chaconas**

illustrated by **Lisa McCue**

VIKING

VIKING
Published by Penguin Group
Penguin Young Readers Group, 345 Hudson Street, New York, New York 10014, U.S.A.
Penguin Group (Canada), 90 Eglinton Avenue East, Suite 700, Toronto, Ontario, Canada M4P 2Y3
(a division of Pearson Penguin Canada Inc.)
Penguin Books Ltd, 80 Strand, London WC2R 0RL, England
Penguin Ireland, 25 St Stephen's Green, Dublin 2, Ireland (a division of Penguin Books Ltd)
Penguin Group (Australia), 250 Camberwell Road, Camberwell, Victoria 3124, Australia
(a division of Pearson Australia Group Pty Ltd)
Penguin Books India Pvt Ltd, 11 Community Centre, Panchsheel Park, New Delhi – 110 017, India
Penguin Group (NZ), 67 Apollo Drive, Rosedale, North Shore 0632, New Zealand
(a division of Pearson New Zealand Ltd)
Penguin Books (South Africa) (Pty) Ltd, 24 Sturdee Avenue, Rosebank, Johannesburg 2196,
South Africa

Penguin Books Ltd, Registered Offices: 80 Strand, London WC2R 0RL, England

First published in 2009 by Viking, a division of Penguin Young Readers Group

· 1 3 5 7 9 10 8 6 4 2

LIBRARY OF CONGRESS CATALOGING-IN-PUBLICATION DATA
Chaconas, Dori
Cork & Fuzz : finders keepers / by Dori Chaconas ; illustrated by Lisa McCue.
p. cm. — (Viking easy-to-read)
Summary: Although Cork the muskrat is short and likes to find things and Fuzz the possum is tall
and likes to keep things, the pair remain best friends even after Fuzz finds Cork's
lost stone and decides to keep it.
ISBN 978-0-670-01113-1 (hardcover)
[1. Best friends—Fiction. 2. Friendship—Fiction. 3. Lost and found possessions—Fiction.
4. Opossums—Fiction. 5. Muskrat—Fiction.] I. McCue, Lisa, ill. II. Title. III. Title: Cork and Fuzz.
IV. Title: Finders keepers.
PZ7.C342Cof 2009
[E]—dc22
2008021551

Manufactured in China
Set in Bookman

Chapter One

Cork was a short muskrat.

He liked to find things.

He liked to find soft feathers,

smooth sticks,

and shiny stones.

For Nicki, finder and keeper

of small things.

—D.C.

To my husband, Ken, I found you, and

you're a keeper!

—L.M.

Fuzz was a tall possum.

He liked to keep things.

He liked to keep food in his mouth,

jokes in his head,

and sometimes

someone else's things.

Two best friends.

Kind of the same, but different.

One day Cork found a shiny green stone.
It was the best stone! He threw it up in
the air. He caught it. He threw it in the air
again. And then he lost it.

"Oh, no!" he said.

He looked in the grass. He looked in the ferns. He looked in the bushes. But he could not find his new green stone.

Fuzz came running.

"Cork! Cork!" Fuzz called. "Hurry! Come to my yard! I have found something!"

"I have lost something!" Cork said. "I have

lost my best green stone."

"How did you lose it?" Fuzz asked.

"I was throwing it up in the air," Cork said.

"I was catching it. I missed! Now I cannot

find it."

Fuzz looked down at his feet. He bent over.

He picked up a shiny green stone.

"Look what I found!" Fuzz said. "I found a green stone."

"That is the stone I lost!" Cork said.

"Finders keepers," Fuzz said.

"But that is my best stone!" Cork said.

"Will you give it back to me?"

"I will think about it," Fuzz said. "But first come to my yard. Come and see what I have found!"

Chapter Two

"What did you find?" Cork asked.

"I found a lump in my yard!" Fuzz said.

"There are a lot of lumps in your yard," Cork said. "Can I have my stone back?"

Fuzz held the stone tighter.

"I did not find an old lump," Fuzz said. "I found a new lump!"

"What does it look like?" Cork asked. "And can I have my stone back, *please*?"

"It is a hidden lump," Fuzz said. "It is hidden under a pile of leaves."

"Maybe it is only a lump of leaves," Cork said. "And *please*, *please*, PLEASE can I have my stone?"

Fuzz held the stone behind his back.

"It is not only a lump of leaves!" Fuzz said.

"There is something under the leaves. It makes a strange noise."

"Do you think you have found something dangerous?" Cork asked.

Fuzz's eyes opened wide.

"We will take a big, long stick!" Fuzz said.

"Just in case."

They found a big, long stick. They ran
back to Fuzz's yard.

"Where is it?" Cork asked.

"There," Fuzz whispered. He pointed at a
pile of leaves.

The pile of leaves wiggled. Something under
the leaves said, *"Chip-chip-chip!"*

Fuzz lifted the stick over his head. "Should
I hit it?" he asked.

"No!" said Cork. "First we need to see if
it is dangerous."

"Okay," said Fuzz. "If it is not dangerous, I
will keep it. If it is dangerous, you can keep it."
Fuzz poked the end of the stick into the pile
of leaves.

"Chip-chip!"

Chomp!

"It chomped the end of the stick!" Fuzz
yelled. "What do I do now?"

"Pull the stick out!" Cork said.

Fuzz pulled the stick out of the leaves. A
small, brown thing hung on the end of the
stick. It hung on with its teeth.

19

Chapter Three

"It is a baby something!" Fuzz said.

"It is not a baby," Cork said.

"It is a chip-mouse."

Fuzz jiggled the stick. The chipmunk

bounced on the end of it.

"He is cute and bouncy," Fuzz said. "I think

I will keep him!"

"You cannot keep a chip-mouse," Cork said.

"I found him," Fuzz said. "I can keep him

for a pet. Finders keepers!"

"Oh, brother!" Cork said.

The chipmunk dropped to the ground.

"Chip-chip-chip!" he said.

He picked up a nut. He stuck it in his cheek.

He picked up a berry. He stuck it in his cheek.

He picked up a seed pod.

He stuck it in his cheek.

"Chip-chip-chip!"

"I wonder how much he can stuff in his
cheeks," Cork said.

23

"We can find out," Fuzz said. "We will help him."

Fuzz handed two nuts to the chipmunk. The chipmunk stuffed them into his cheeks.

Cork handed three berries to the chipmunk. The chipmunk stuffed them into his cheeks.

The chipmunk's cheeks grew fatter and fatter.

"Wow!" Fuzz said. He opened his paw to pick up another nut. The shiny green stone fell to the ground. The chipmunk scooped it up and stuffed it into his cheek.

"Wait!" Fuzz yelled. "That is my stone!"

"That is *my* stone!" Cork said.

"Chip-chip-chip!" said the chipmunk.

"I think he is saying 'finders keepers,'" Cork said.

The chipmunk disappeared under his lump of leaves with his cheeks full of nuts and berries and the shiny green stone.

Chapter Four

The chipmunk popped out of the leaves
with empty cheeks. He ran back to the
nut tree.

"Now my stone has chip-mouse spit on it,"
Cork said.

"I want it back anyway," Fuzz said.

Cork and Fuzz dug into the lump of leaves.

They found nuts and berries and seeds.

And they found the shiny green stone.

Fuzz grabbed it.

"Finders keepers," he said.

"CHIP-CHIP-CHIP-CHIP-CHIP!" the chipmunk yelled at them. He jumped up and down. He ran in circles, flicking his tail.

"I think he is mad at us," Fuzz said.

"I think we should go home now,"
Cork said.

Fuzz looked back at the chattering
chipmunk. He sniffled.

"I wanted to keep that chip-mouse for a
pet," Fuzz said. "Now I feel sad."

Cork put his arm around his friend's
shoulders.

"Sometimes we cannot keep the things we
find," Cork said. "Sometimes they belong to
someone else."

"Who does the chip-mouse belong to?"
Fuzz asked.

"Well," said Cork, "I guess he just
belongs to himself."

Fuzz looked at the green stone in his paw.
He gave it to Cork.

"You are right," Fuzz said. "I cannot keep your green stone, either. Now I feel sadder." Cork patted Fuzz on the back. "You can borrow my stone sometime," he said. "And if it will make you feel better, we can see how many nuts we can stuff into our own cheeks."

31

And so they did. Two best friends,

arm in arm, heading for home with

fat, fat cheeks.